Boing-Boing

the Bionic Cat

Boing-Boing
the Bionic Cat

by Larry L. Hench

Illustrations by Ruth Denise Lear

Published by
The American Ceramic Society
735 Ceramic Place
Westerville, Ohio 43081 USA

The American Ceramic Society
735 Ceramic Place
Westerville, Ohio 43081
www.ceramics.org

Printed in Hong Kong.
First edition.
09 08 07 06 05 04 03 02 01 00   10 9 8 7 6 5 4 3 2 1

The text of this book is set in Koch Plain. The illustrations are watercolor and ink.
This book was printed on acid-free paper and was Smyth-sewn with cotton thread.

Senior Director, Publications
Mark Mecklenborg

Marketing Assistant
Jennifer Brewer

Acquisitions
Mary J. Cassells

Production Manager
John Wilson

Development
Sarah Godby

Design
Rodger Wilson
KPI Design, Columbus, Ohio

Library of Congress Cataloging-in-Publication Data

Hench, L.L.
    Boing-Boing the Bionic Cat / Larry L. Hench; illustrated by Ruth Denise Lear. -- 1st ed.
        p. cm.
    Summary: Daniel, who loves cats but is allergic to them, is delighted when his inventive neighbor Professor George builds him a bionic cat with fiber-optic fur, computer-controlled joints, electronic eyes, and ceramic-sensor whiskers.
    ISBN: 1-57498-109-9 (hc.)
    [1. Cats--Fiction. 2. Robots--Fiction. 3. Inventors--Fiction.] I. Lear, Ruth Denise, ill. II. Title.

PZ7.H37765 Bo 2000
[Fic]--dc21
                                                99-058988

For more information about The American Ceramic Society or its publications, please call (614) 794-5890 or visit <www.ceramics.org>.

For Daniel, who read it first.

Contents

BIONIC CAT
DESIGN FEATURES

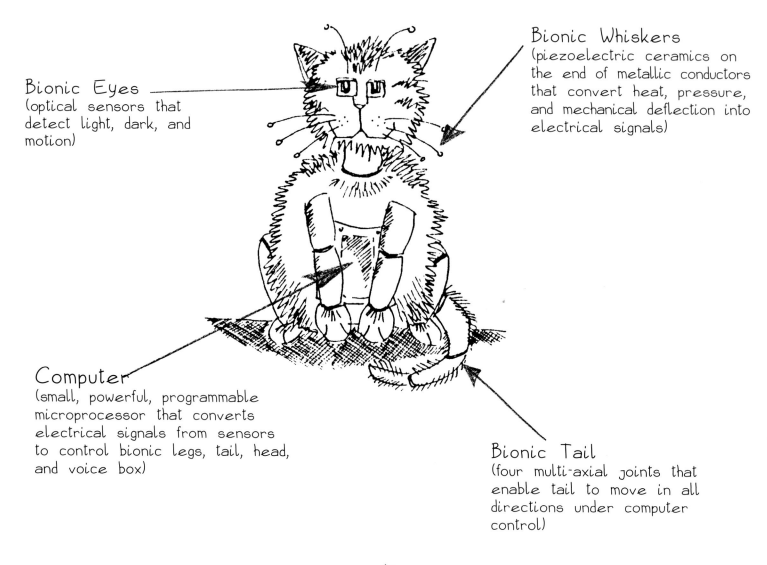

Bionic Eyes
(optical sensors that detect light, dark, and motion)

Bionic Whiskers
(piezoelectric ceramics on the end of metallic conductors that convert heat, pressure, and mechanical deflection into electrical signals)

Computer
(small, powerful, programmable microprocessor that converts electrical signals from sensors to control bionic legs, tail, head, and voice box)

Bionic Tail
(four multi-axial joints that enable tail to move in all directions under computer control)

BIONIC CAT
DESIGN FEATURES

Fiber-Optic Fur
(optical glass fiber, covering over all surfaces, that transmits sunlight through the fibers to photoelectric cells that charge the batteries)

Batteries
(6 rechargeable 9-volt batteries that provide power to the computer, the bionic eyes, tail, legs, head, and ceramic heating elements)

Bionic Voice Box
(programmable voice simulator activated by sensors embedded in the fiber-optic fur; controlled by the computer)

Bionic Legs
(4 legs with 3 multi-axial joints per leg connected to small motors controlled by the computer)

Chapter One

Daniel was sitting on the front steps of his house with his head in his hands.

He wiped away a tear that dripped down his cheek as he remembered his mother's words of a few minutes earlier.

"Daniel, I've told you for the last time you cannot have a cat! Now run outside and play and stop bothering me. I've got work to do! I have had it right up to here about cats!" she said, holding her hand up to her neck.

But Daniel had said, "Why not, Mummy? I promise to take care of it. I really will. I promise. I promise," he pleaded.

His mother sighed a great big sigh, "Daniel, if I've told you once, I've told you a million times: you cannot have a cat because you are allergic to them.

"Every time you pet a cat you start sneezing and get red blotches all over you.

"The doctor says if you have a cat your allergy will only get worse."

Daniel was sad because he knew his mother was right. "She's always right," he grumbled.

Just then Daniel looked up and saw his neighbor, Professor George, walking up the road.

"What's the matter, Dan?" Professor George asked. "You sure do look miserable."

"I am, Professor George," Daniel answered. "My mum won't let me have a cat."

"That's too bad," replied the professor. "Why not? Does she think you won't take care of it?"

"No," answered Daniel. "It's because I'm allergic to cats. They make me sneeze and break out in red spots when I pet them.

"I guess I'll just never have a cat," Daniel moaned.

"Well, I don't know about that," Professor George said. "Never say never. Many things change for the better with time. Just be patient, Dan," he said. "Maybe something will happen so you can have a cat someday."

Professor George had the beginning of an idea. He started whistling as he walked on home, letting the idea grow in more and more detail.

By the time he got home, Professor George knew what he was going to do. He was going to build Daniel a bionic cat. "It will be like some of the robots we build in my lab," he thought. "But, Dan's bionic cat must also be like a real cat. That is a good challenge."

Professor George was no ordinary professor. He gave lectures and taught students about bioengineering and went to meetings, just like the other professors at the big university nearby; however, Professor George was also head of an engineering research laboratory at the university.

His laboratory was very special. He and his students did research and built robots. Their robots were not at all like the robots in the movies. They were robots used to make cars, trains, and big machines.

For relaxation, Professor George liked to spend time in the workshop in his basement at home. It wasn't any ordinary workshop, though. He had all sorts of tools and electronic gadgets. He also had a computer connected to the big Super Computer at the university.

Professor George gave his wife a quick kiss when he got home, then he went straight down to his workshop. "Call me when dinner is ready, honey," he said. "I'm going to work on a little project, for Dan next door."

He sat down at his computer and connected it to the Super Computer. He quickly did some calculations. Then he did some design drawings on the computer. When he was finished, Professor George leaned back and stretched with a big smile on his face and chuckled. "It looks like it can be done," he said.

Chapter Two

After a quick dinner and apologies to his wife, Professor George went back downstairs to his workshop. He started building a little robot. He worked on and on. It got later and later.

His wife came down to the workshop and said, as she gave him a kiss good night, "George, you can stay up all night if you want to, but I am going to bed. Good night."

"Good night, honey," Professor George answered. "It shouldn't take too much longer. I want to finish now that I'm this far along."

Unfortunately, he was wrong. The sun was just coming up when Professor George stretched and said to himself with a big yawn, "Oh boy, I think it's finally finished."

He got up from his workbench and rubbed his eyes. He looked down at what was sitting there looking up at him. "It sure looks real," he said to himself, with a smile. "It looks just like a bionic cat."

The little robot was just the size of a cat. It had four legs that could move with battery power, and light-yellow electronic eyes that told the little computer inside its belly where it was going.

It even had whiskers on either side of a little nose. The whiskers ended with tiny little electronic ceramic sensors that also were connected to the little computer inside. When the whiskers touch something they send a signal to the little computer, telling the bionic cat to move around the object.

It had a tail that moved. But, best of all, the bionic cat had fur. Its fur was very, very special. It was fiber-optic fur.

The fiber-optic fur soaks up the sunshine when the bionic cat sits in the window, as cats like to do. The sunlight travels down the glass fibers to the inside of the cat where it is changed into electricity by a solar cell.

"Let's check out your fiber-optic fur, little fellow," said Professor George as he put a special bulb in his desk lamp. He shone the lamp onto the bionic cat.

"Now, let's see whether the light is charging your batteries," he said as he looked at the meter hooked up to the inside of the bionic cat.

"Good, it's nine volts, that's just right," Professor George said. "The electricity will keep your batteries charged. You can act just like a real cat. You can sit and catnap in the sunshine during the day. That will charge your batteries. Then, if you want to, you can run around all night."

Professor George was very pleased with his creation, in spite of being very sleepy. He had enjoyed building the bionic cat almost as much as he enjoyed teaching his engineering students.

He picked up the bionic cat and said to himself as he gently stroked its fur, "Well, it does feel real—just what I was hoping for. If you can't pet a cat, you might as well not have one."

Next, he felt under the bionic cat's belly and switched on the batteries. "Let's see how you work, little fellow," he said as he stroked the fur. The eyes lit up with a very pleasant soft yellow glow. The pupils in the eyes got smaller when a lot of light shone on them. They opened wide when there was only a little bit of light. "So far, so good," Professor George said to the bionic cat.

Next he lightly stroked the fur. The bionic cat responded with a very pleasing "Purrr, purrr, purrr," from its mouth and the small voice simulator located in its throat.

"That sounds just right," Professor George responded.

"Now, let's see how you get around," he said as he set the bionic cat down on the floor. Immediately the cat started wandering around the cluttered workshop with its tail switching back and forth.

When the bionic cat got close to a pile of books, some of its whiskers warned it to walk around them.

When it got close to the electric heater sitting on the floor, its whiskers warned it electronically, "Too hot. Too hot," and the bionic cat backed away from the heater.

"Very good. Very, very good job, kitty," chuckled Professor George. "I think you'll do fine, just fine indeed. I can't wait to see Dan's face when he sees you.

"Well, I think that is everything," Professor George said to himself. "All systems seem to be working properly. I'd better rush. I have a class to teach in two hours and I need a hot shower and some breakfast to wake me up."

Chapter Three

Just as he was leaving the workshop, Professor George remembered one more thing. "Oh no," he said. "I forgot to check to see if the bionic cat can speak."

So, he picked up the cat and switched on its batteries. He rubbed the bionic cat's nose and stroked its fur at the same time and it said "Boing-Boing!"

Professor George was so startled he almost dropped the cat. He quickly tried again, rubbing the nose a little more gently and stroking the fur in a different place.

Once again the bionic cat said "Boing-Boing."

He repeated this a third and fourth time. The result was still the same. The bionic cat always said "𝕭𝕠𝕚𝕟𝕘-𝕭𝕠𝕚𝕟𝕘."

"Oh no!" exclaimed Professor George. "I must have messed up when I programmed the voice section of the computer this morning. That's what happens when you try to do too much when you're tired and sleepy. You're sure to mess up somewhere."

"Oh well," he said with a big sigh. "I'll have to wait until I get home to fix it. I have to get to class now. There just isn't enough time. Dan will just have to wait another day for his cat."

Chapter Four

Later that afternoon, Professor George was slowly walking home from the university, yawning at almost every step. It was hard to stay awake after working all night on the bionic cat.

Once again, he saw Daniel sitting on the front steps of his house. This time Daniel was crying. Professor George stopped and asked, "Dan, why are you crying? Is it about not having a cat?"

"No," Daniel blubbered. "I wish it were. It's about my mum. She's sick in bed with the flu. The doctor says she has a temperature and is really ill. He says that I have to be very quiet. I wish I had some way to cheer her up."

Professor George said, "I have something that will cheer up both of you. Come home with me and I'll show you."

Daniel smiled. Professor George
always had surprises at his house.
There were lots of tools and
computer games. And best of all,
it seemed, his wife always had
something baking.

Daniel was right. When they
arrived she gave him a big chocolate
cookie and a glass of milk.

"Come down to my workshop and
see what's here," Professor George
called from the basement.

Daniel jumped down the steps,
three at a time. He looked around
the room. He could hardly believe his eyes. In the
middle of Professor George's worktable was a cat.

It did not look like any other cat, though. Its fur was shiny. You could almost see through the fur.

But the cat was not moving.

Daniel asked, "Is it a real cat, Professor George?"

"Well, it's sort of real," answered the Professor. "Here, I'll show you."

"See, it's a bionic cat," Professor George said as he showed Daniel how to turn it on with the switch under its tummy. "I built it from many of the electronic and ceramic materials we use in my research lab, Dan."

Daniel could hardly believe his eyes when the bionic cat's eyes began to glow. "Hey, its tail is switching back and forth just like a real cat. And feel! It's starting to get warm," Daniel said.

"Wow! How does that happen?" Daniel asked.

"The bionic cat has low-power ceramic heating elements inside that make it feel warm. In fact, it is designed to be at the same temperature as a real cat," answered Professor George.

"What else does it do?" asked Daniel.

"Put it on the floor and watch," replied the Professor.

Daniel put the bionic cat on the floor and looked up in surprise.

"Just look at it go!" exclaimed Daniel. "It walks like a real cat. You can hardly tell the difference.

"Wow!" shouted Daniel. "Look how it dodges right around the table legs.

"Hey, it doesn't run into the heater either! How does it know how to do all those things?" asked Daniel.

So, Professor George told him about the whiskers and the sensors. "These are very special types of ceramic materials, Dan. They are able to convert heat or motion into electrical signals to control the cat. It is like the nerves in your fingers sending signals to your brain that something you touch is either hot or cold."

"So that is why it's a bionic cat," Daniel replied. "It has electronic controls that are like a real cat's biological controls."

"Great, Dan," responded Professor George. "That is exactly right. You learn very quickly."

He then showed Daniel the little computer inside the bionic cat's tummy. "It is very small so it does not use much energy, Dan," explained Professor George.

Next, Professor George said, "Here, you hold it and stroke its fur, Dan. But you must be very gentle because it is fiber-optic fur." He explained how the light travels down the fur and recharges the batteries when the cat sits in the sunlight.

Daniel was very gentle as he stroked the fur.

"Listen!" he exclaimed. "Listen, it's purring. It's saying 'purrr, purrr, purrr,' just like a real cat. That is really fantastic! How does it do that?"

So Professor George showed Daniel the tiny little voice box, and told him all about programming the little computer to activate the voice box when the fur was stroked. Then he remembered.

"**OH NO!**" Professor George shouted in dismay. "I forgot all about the mistake I was going to fix before I showed you the bionic cat!"

Daniel asked, a little frightened, "What's wrong Professor George? What's the matter? Everything looks all right to me. The bionic cat is fantastic. What's bothering you so much?"

Professor George answered, "Here, I'll show you. This morning I was so sleepy that I made a mistake when I was programming the last part of the computer.

"Let your thumb rub the cat's nose at the same time as you stroke its fur and see what happens, Dan," said the Professor.

Daniel did as he was told and immediately the bionic cat said "**Boing-Boing!**"

Daniel laughed loudly. "It said 'Boing-Boing!' That's really funny. What's so bad about that, Professor George?"

Professor George answered, "It's supposed to say 'Meow-Meow, Meow-Meow.' All cats say 'Meow-Meow.' The computer will have to be reprogrammed to make it perfect."

Daniel replied, "But Professor George, this isn't just any old cat. This is a bionic cat. You just told me so yourself a little while ago. It's perfectly OK for a bionic cat to say 'Boing-Boing' instead of 'Meow-Meow.' In fact, it seems just right for it to say 'Boing-Boing.' That makes it even more special."

"You mean you're not disappointed, Dan, because it says 'Boing-Boing'?" Professor George asked.

"Of course not!" Daniel replied. "That makes the cat even better."

Professor George was surprised. He thought that everything had to be perfect to be appreciated. Maybe he was wrong about that.

"You would like the cat just as it is?" Professor George asked Daniel.

"What? You mean it can be mine?" shouted Daniel. "WOW! Are you serious?"

"Of course," replied the Professor. "I made it especially for you. Look at your arms. You have been holding it for awhile now. Do you see any red blotches? Have you been sneezing? Are your eyes watering?"

"Can I take it home now to show Mum?" Daniel asked. "I'll bet it will cheer her up a lot."

"Of course you can," said Professor George, yawning. "What are you going to call it? Every cat has to have a name—even a bionic cat."

"Oh, that's easy," said Daniel. "I'll call it 'Boing-Boing the Bionic Cat.' And every time it talks it will say its name, 'Boing-Boing'."

"That sounds good to me," said the Professor, anxious to lie down for a nap.

Daniel ran home as fast as he could, carrying Boing-Boing with him.

He was right—for as soon as he told his mother about Professor George and showed her the bionic cat and the wonderful things it could do, she began to feel better. And, when she rubbed the cat's nose and stroked its silky fiber-optic fur and it said "Boing-Boing" she laughed and laughed. Then, Daniel knew she was going to be just fine.

The End

Maybe yes and maybe no . . .

. . . only time will tell!

About the Author

Larry L. Hench, Ph.D., served as professor of ceramic engineering for 32 years at The University of Florida, and is currently professor of ceramic materials at Imperial College of Science, Technology, and Medicine at the University of London and director of the Imperial College Centre for Tissue Regeneration and Repair.

A world-renowned scientist, graduate of The Ohio State University, and Fellow of The American Ceramic Society—Hench's numerous achievements, honors, scholarly writings, and patents, over his 40-year career, span several fields including: ceramics, glass and glass-ceramic materials, radiation damage, nuclear waste solidification, advanced optical materials, origins of life, ethics, technology transfer, and bioceramics applications and mechanisms. He is credited with the discovery of Bioglass®, the first man-made material to bond to living bone—helping millions of people; and he continues to discover new applications in bioceramics for this amazing material. Hench is currently working with students to find the genes that are activated by bioactive glasses and ceramics. Once these genes are found, he hopes to develop preventive treatments to stop deterioration of bones in people as they grow older.

His children's books extend his love of teaching, and science and engineering to a new generation. Everything built into the stories is scientifically valid and could be done. The inspiration for these books comes from his nine grandchildren.

Hench, an Ohio native, now divides his time between London and the United States. He and his wife, June Wilson, share four children and nine grandchildren.

About the illustrator

Ruth Denise Lear was born in Wilmslow, Cheshire, England, in 1965, and lives now with her husband and three children in a rural village on the outskirts of Macclesfield, Cheshire.

Her love of drawing began in childhood and has never left her. If there is a blank sheet of paper around she cannot resist doodling on it.

BOING-BOING THE BIONIC CAT is her first book, and she couldn't be more excited about it. Ruth says, "It is particularly apt that it should be about a cat, as I've always loved them very much—both wild and domestic; although I've never seen a bionic cat!" Not until now, anyway.

Forthcoming!

In subsequent books in the series, Daniel and Boing-Boing the Bionic Cat become an invincible duo. Each story involves an adventure, a new part for Boing-Boing (giving the cat surprising new capabilities!), and Daniel and Boing-Boing to the rescue! Don't be surprised to learn of Daniel and Boing-Boing thwarting a jewel thief or rescuing someone from an Egyptian tomb. Where will their next adventure be?

About The American Ceramic Society

The American Ceramic Society (ACerS) serves its members and the worldwide ceramic community by promoting the development and use of ceramics through forums for knowledge exchange.

As the world's leading organization dedicated to the advancement of ceramics, ACerS serves more than 10,000 members and subscribers in 80 countries. ACerS' members include ceramic engineers, scientists, researchers, educators, students, sales and production personnel, manufacturers, and others in the ceramics and related materials industry. Founded in 1898, ACerS provides the latest technical, scientific, and educational information to its members and other constituencies.